# SMALL FOOT

# When Migo
# Met Smallfoot

Adapted by Tina Gallo
Illustrated by Art Baltazar

Ready-to-Read

Simon Spotlight
New York   London   Toronto   Sydney   New Delhi

SISC41042

SIMON SPOTLIGHT
An imprint of Simon & Schuster Children's Publishing Division
1230 Avenue of the Americas, New York, New York 10020
This Simon Spotlight edition August 2018
All rights reserved, including the right of reproduction in whole or in part in any form.
SIMON SPOTLIGHT, READY-TO-READ, and colophon are registered trademarks of Simon & Schuster, Inc.
For information about special discounts for bulk purchases, please contact Simon & Schuster Special Sales
at 1-866-506-1949 or business@simonandschuster.com.
Manufactured in the United States of America 0718 LAK
10 9 8 7 6 5 4 3 2 1
ISBN 978-1-5344-3173-7 (hc)
ISBN 978-1-5344-3172-0 (pbk)
ISBN 978-1-5344-3174-4 (eBook)

Hi! I'm Migo.
I am a Yeti.
It's nice to meet you!
I have an amazing story to tell you.

I live with my dad.
We live in this beautiful village.

Everything here
is perfect.

Nothing ever changes.
We like it that way!
At least . . . we thought we did.

We must follow the laws
in our village.
They are written in stone
and worn by our leader,
the Stonekeeper.

We do not question
these laws.
They are actually written in stone!
Take a closer look. . . .

One stone shows us
that our world is an island.
The island floats on a sea of clouds.
Below those clouds is
the Great Nothing.

The Stonekeeper
has a very important job.
He reads and interprets
the stones for us.
The stones also tell us
there is no such thing
as a Smallfoot!

Sometimes I have questions
for the Stonekeeper.
But he says
he is trying to keep
the village safe.

So when I have questions,
I keep them to myself.

I try not to think about them.
Sooner or later they go away.

But I always feel better
when I ask my friends and family
about the questions.

One day I saw a Smallfoot fall from a shiny flying machine.
I even saw his small foot and boot!
I told the Stonekeeper about it.
He said it was probably a yak.

Then I heard about
a secret group.
The group included
other Yetis like me
who wanted to prove
that the Smallfoot exists!

Meechee is the Stonekeeper's
daughter and a member of the group.
(I have a little crush on her.
Don't tell anybody.)
The group showed me
objects they had found.

The objects made them believe
that Smallfoot was real.
They showed me a tiny boot.
It was just like the one I saw!

I showed them where
my Smallfoot went—
the Great Nothing below.
Meechee wanted me
to look for the Smallfoot.
I was scared, but I went down
to the Great Nothing.

That is where I met
my new friend.
I was looking for a Smallfoot.
He was looking for a Yeti.
We found each other!

I thought he was going to
be scary, but he was adorable!
It seemed like he was
playing with me.

I couldn't wait to bring him back to my village!
It got too cold for him on the way there.
I took him to a cave.
I tried to warm him up, but that scared him.

I tried to feed him.
That scared him too!

We weren't alone in the cave.
An angry mama bear
was already there.
I kept her talking
while my Smallfoot friend escaped.

Then my foot got stuck
in a bear trap.
He helped me
get my foot out.

I think that is when
we became friends.
I carried him back to my village.
I was a hero when I returned
with the Smallfoot!
Almost everyone was excited
to see him.
They had so many questions.
The Stonekeeper did not believe
it was a Smallfoot.
He wanted to consult the stones.
My Smallfoot did not
understand anything we said.

Then Meechee and Smallfoot
found a way to communicate.
They used drawings.
But the Smallfoot couldn't stay
with us.
The mountain was too cold for him.

I did not want him to go.
But it was for the best.
Meechee decided to bring him
back to his home.

I wish I could spend more time
with my friend Smallfoot.
I have so many questions.
Now I know it is good
to ask for answers.
Who knows?
Maybe someday we will meet again.